First published in 1986 in German by
Verlag Heinrich Ellermann, München
as *Der Rote Handschuh.*

© 1986 Verlag Heinrich Ellermann, München.

English adaptation © 1986, Silver Burdett Company,
Morristown, New Jersey.

ISBN 0-382-09379-8
Library of Congress Catalog Card Number 86-42824

First published in the United States in 1986 by
Silver Burdett Company,
Morristown, New Jersey.

Published simultaneously in Canada by
GLC/Silver Burdett Publishers,
Agincourt, Ontario.

Printed in West Germany.

Tilde Michels

The Red Mitten

Illustrations by Winfried Opgenoorth
English adaptation by Lindamichellebaron

Silver Burdett Company
Morristown, New Jersey • Agincourt, Ontario

A bright red mitten lying here,
Deserted and lonely, only half of a pair.
It looks strange in the forest, lost on the land,
Instead of being worn on somebody's hand.

A buck finds the patch of red not too far from his feet,
He can't wait, he thinks it's something good to eat.
He walks closer . . . ready, how good it should taste,
But the smell lets him know his walk was a waste.
So he snorts . . . he is angry, he's been hungry all day,
He pokes the thing with his antlers and flings it away.

The mitten seems to fly right through the air,
And unexpectedly lands before Mother Hare.
What, she wonders, can she do with that?
Maybe it will make a soft, warm hat.
But the mitt won't fit little rabbit's long ears,
So he casts it away after many tugs and tears.

A butterfly flits through grass and trees,
And lights on the "red flower" he sees.
It should have a delicious nectar, he thinks,
So he attempts to sip a few drinks.
As you can imagine, the mitten is dry,
Disappointed, he flits his way back to the sky.

A raven sees the red fluffy patch,
And thinks it's an animal he can catch.
He dives toward it with his beaked mouth,
He'll take it with him on his trip to the south.
Unhappy, he doesn't like what he's found,
So he drops the mitten in a pond on the ground.

Two ducks find the wet red toy,
Now they can play with it, what a joy!
Except they don't know how to share,
So they tug and pull and rip and tear.
Finally tired, they waddle to the land,
And leave the mitten behind in the sand.

The ragged, red mitten lies there,
Deserted and lonely, only half of a pair.

Freezing and frightened, missing its hand,
It's covered by winter, left alone on the land.

After several long sad months ice by,
Bright sunlight smiles through the sky.
Something red seems to take a peek,
It looks like our friend playing hide and seek.
Yes! Our friend made it to another season,
But why? Our mitt wonders. For what reason?

The answer doesn't take too long,
It flies in with a pair of birds' desperate song.
"We need a nest for our eggs to rest.
We need a nest and we want the best."

They dance and sing when they spy the mitten,
Torn and tattered, where frost had bitten.
They usually use twigs and sticks and stuff,
Which serves the purpose, but it's so rough.
They can use this soft red thread,
To make a most comfortable family bed.

They build their red nest on the branch of a tree,
It is soft and comfortable, they sing happily.
"We have a nest for our eggs to rest.
We have a nest and we have the best!"

No longer deserted and lonely, only half of a pair,
The mitten has a purpose now — lining a home in the air!

There are other stories about lost red mittens. One is illustrated on the next few pages. You can make up your own story to go with the pictures . . .

1

2

3

4

5

6

7

8

9

10

Which ending do you like best? This one?

11

Or this one?

12